IMAGINE THAT

Licensed exclusively to Imagine That Publishing Ltd
Tide Mill Way, Woodbridge, Suffolk, IP12 1AP, UK
www.imaginethat.com
Copyright © 2014 Imagine That Group Ltd
All rights reserved
0 2 4 6 8 9 7 5 3 1
Manufactured in China

Written by Oakley Graham
Illustrated by Patricia Yuste

ISBN 978-1-78244-435-0

A catalogue record for this book is available from the British Library

The Moon Flower Fairies

'For Isadora'
Oakley Graham

When the moon is full on a warm midsummer night,
Moon flowers open their petals and reveal a wondrous sight.

Whilst every man, woman and child is fast asleep,
Moon Flower Fairies are born without a peep.

The newborn fairies doze on their petal beds,
Until a wisp of wind wakes their sleepy heads.

They stretch their wings in the pale moonlight,
Then spring into the air on their maiden flight.

Sprinkling fairy dust as they laugh and sing,
Moon Flower Fairies dance in
magical toadstool rings.

They help to look after the
plants, trees and flowers,
And provide them with shelter
from the wind and showers.

Friendly woodland creatures help the fairies get dressed,
For their magical adventure they want to look their best.

Then a shooting star appears in the moonlit sky,
Towards the light, the Moon Flower Fairies fly.

The star stops above a castle high in the clouds,
A place where no boys or girls are ever allowed.

The fairies arrive on the stroke of midnight,
Bathed in the moonlight, it's a magical sight.

In the cloud castle, whilst you and I are fast asleep,
Moon Flower Fairies weave sweet dreams for us to keep.

Sweet dreams ...

Magical Fairy Facts

Flower Fairies
Flower fairies are good fairies who love to dance and sing. Hiding at the bottom of your garden, fluttering in the woods or sleeping under a toadstool, flower fairies are very shy and you have to be very lucky to see them.

Fairy Names
Flower fairies are usually named after their favourite flowers, such as Rose, Buttercup and Daisy. They use their magical fairy dust to help the plants, trees and flowers grow.

Naughty Fairies
There are many different types of fairy. Elves, goblins, sprites and imps are all types of fairy folk. Many of these are naughty fairies since they often play tricks and cause trouble.

Fairy Spotting
The best time to see fairies is at sunrise, at sunset, when it is misty, on the night of a full moon and on a clear, starry night.

Fairy Holidays
March 25th and September 30th are special fairy holidays. The fairy queen holds magical, moonlight balls to celebrate.

The Little People
The word 'fairy' is French and only came to mean 'small, magical people' about 600 years ago. Before that, all fairy folk were called 'elves'. People used to be very scared of bad fairies, like goblins and leprechauns, so they called good fairies 'The Little People' or 'The Good People' instead.